Events of the Revolution

The Battle for
Long Island & New York

by Susan and John Lee

illustrated by Tom Dunnington

 CHILDRENS PRESS, CHICAGO

Library of Congress Cataloging in Publication Data

Lee, Susan.
    The battle for Long Island and New York.

    (Events of the Revolution)
    SUMMARY: Unwilling to side with either the rebels
or loyalists, two young brothers make up their minds
when they become involved in the Battle of Long Island.
    [1. United States—History—Revolution, 1775-1783—
Fiction] I. Lee, John, joint author. II. Dunnington,
Tom, ill. III. Title.
PZ7.L51487Bat   [E]   74-23988
ISBN 0-516-04671-3

Chapter 1
EAST RIVER CANNON

"Let me take the ship into New York this time," begged Ned.

"No," said Father, "give the tiller to Luke."

"But you let me take her sometimes."

"Aye," said Father, "but this load of flour cost a lot of money. You'll get to sail the ship later."

Ned gave the tiller to Luke. Then he moved to
sit by his father. "We'll always stay together,
won't we?" he asked.

"Aye, Ned," Father said, "with your mother
gone, we need each other."

"I'm eight," said Ned. "And Luke is fourteen.
We need you."

Father laughed. "And I need you boys."

"This flour should bring us good money in New York," said Father. "General Washington is buying all the food he can get."

"Yes, sir," said Luke, "it's good Westchester flour. There's none better."

"You know a lot," said Ned, "but only because you heard Father say it."

"That's one good way to learn," said Luke.

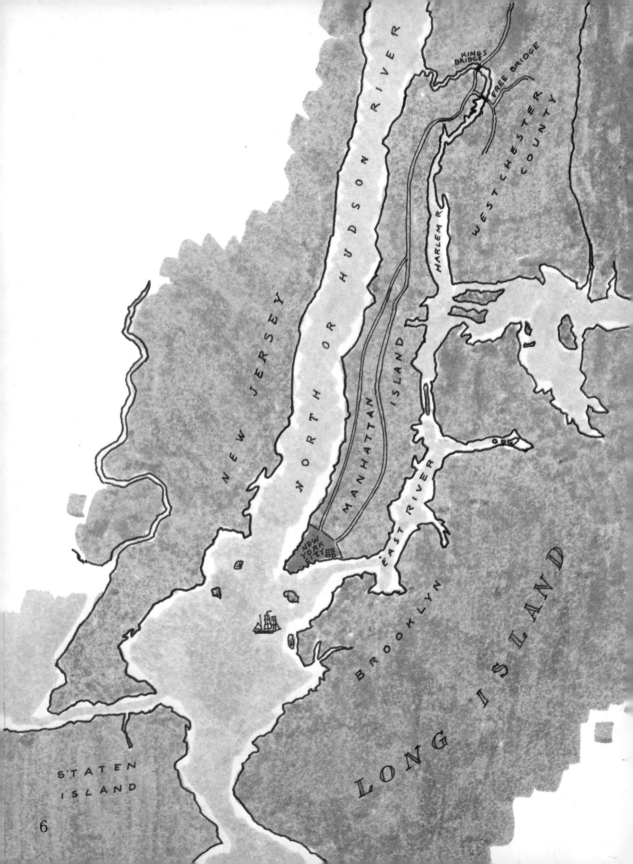

"Luke!" said Father. "Tend to your sailing. We don't want to end up in Brooklyn. Bring the *London Lady* up to Murray's Wharf. We'll sell the flour there."

"Yes, sir," said Luke.

"Tell me again, Father," begged Luke. "Why did you name our ship the *London Lady*?"

"Because your mother was a London Lady," the father said. "She was born in London. Came to New York when she was small. We got married here. But she always talked of going back to London. When she died I named the ship the *London Lady*. It seemed to me that she would have liked that."

"Was she pretty?" asked Ned.

"She was," said his father. "Small too, like this ship. And always fun to be with. Like this ship."

Luke worked the ship up to Murray's Wharf. "Someone unloaded coffee today," he said, "I can smell it."

"New lumber there, too," said his father. "You can smell the pine in the air."

"Look!" yelled Ned. "Look at that cannon!"

"Where?" said Luke. "Where's the cannon?"

Ned pointed at a house. "Right there," he said, "in that hole in the street."

"Yup," said his father. "Washington and his rebels are going to fight to keep New York."

Chapter 2
WALL STREET

"Do I have to stay here?" asked Ned.

"One of us must stay," said Father. "I'm going to New Jersey for more flour. I'll need Luke to help me load the flour."

"What's my job?" asked Ned.

"I want you to find Mr. Rose. He'll be somewhere on Wall Street. Tell him we will be back this afternoon with the flour."

Ned walked up Wall Street to the Merchants Coffee House. He saw his friend George Chester across the street. "Ho, George," he yelled. "What are you doing down here?"

"Shhh," went George. "I'm watching the rebels. I'll bet they are planning against our king."

"Come on, George," said Ned, "let's go fishing in the North River."

"No, I don't want to go over there," said George. "There's a gang of rebel boys over there. They'll beat us up."

"Not me," said Ned. "I don't take sides. My father says taking sides in a war is dumb." He hit George on the arm. "Come on, friend, let's go fishing."

"No," said George. "They know I'm loyal to the King. They'll beat me up."

George went up to Water Street, looking both ways for rebels. Ned walked over to the Coffee House. A rough-looking man sat on a stool by the door. Ned looked at him for a time. "Are you a sailor?" Ned asked.

"Yup," said the man.

"So am I," said Ned. "My name's Ned Niles. I sail on the *London Lady*."

"Uh huh," said the sailor. "I'm Jacob Smith. I saw your ship down at Murray's Wharf. So you sail on her?"

"Yup," said Ned, trying to sound like the sailor. "Did you see the cannon down there?"

"Yup," said Jacob with a smile. "I'm the gunner for that cannon. Some of us Salem boys came down from Massachusetts with the General."

"You think there'll be a war?" asked Ned.

Jacob smiled. "There was fighting up in Boston. There'll be fighting down here. I didn't come to New York just to watch the pigs in the street."

"My father says there won't be a war here."

"Boy," said Jacob, "you better hope your Pa is right. Comes a war and he won't be sailing much here. Unless the English impress him. Then he'll be sailing on an English ship."

"What's impress mean?" asked Ned.

"That means the English grab you off your ship and put you on an English ship."

"Not my father! He's not a rebel," cried Ned as he turned away.

Meanwhile the *London Lady* sailed down the
East River past the end of the island. Luke
moved the tiller, and the ship cut into the North
River.

"Brooklyn on one side. New York on the
other. East River in between. Which will the
English try to take?" asked Father.

"Brooklyn!" answered Luke.

"Why?" his father asked.

"Long Island has the best places to land soldiers. Washington can't watch the shores everywhere," said Luke.

"Good thinking. Anything else?"

Luke took his time before he said anything. His father was a careful man with words. He wanted his sons to think before they said something. "If the English get the big island, they get the farms. And if they get the farms, that will help feed their soldiers."

"Umm," went his father, "got your thinking cap on today, haven't you?"

Luke smiled. He liked it when his father said he was a good thinker.

"Keep close to New York side, boy." Father looked at the fleet of English ships. "Must be over a hundred of the King's ships there. We don't want one of them coming after us."

Luke moved the *Lady* into the North River. "New Jersey," he said, "here we come."

As Luke spoke, a small, fast English ship moved to cut in front of the *London Lady*.

Chapter 3
LOYALISTS AND REBELS

Ned found Mr. Rose in the Coffee House. He took off his hat and stood by the table.

"Hello, Ned," said Mr. Rose. "What are you doing in this den of rebels."

"I came to see you, sir," said Ned. "Father said to tell you he'd have your flour this afternoon."

"Good, good," said Mr. Rose. "That's good news. Does this mean he has joined us rebels?"

"No, I don't think so," said Ned.

"Your father should think about it. We are going to run every loyalist out of New York! Most of them are gone now!"

Ned saw the smile on Mr. Rose's face. But Mr. Rose's voice scared him.

"We aren't loyalists, sir," he said.

"You aren't rebels and you aren't loyalists. You aren't for King George. And you aren't for General George. Your father is sitting on the fence. But soon, very soon, he will have to get down off that fence."

"Yes, sir," said Ned. "I'll tell him."

"And you tell him that if he doesn't stand with us, he stands against us."

"Yes, sir," said Ned as he moved for the door. "I'll tell him what you said."

Ned ran west on Wall Street. At Broadway he turned north. He ran until he came to the Chester house. Mr. Chester loaded two chairs onto his wagon. "You boys say good-bye now," he said, "it's time we headed for Westchester County."

"I wish you didn't have to go," said Ned.

"I wish you were going, too," said George.

"Father says we won't take sides," said Ned.

19

"Ned," said Mr. Chester, "you tell your father I said he is wrong. Sooner or later, he'll have to jump for one George or the other. Tell him to stick with the English King. Your father is English. You are English. The English are going to win. That's as plain as the nose on your face."

"I'll tell him," said Ned. "But he will do what he thinks is best."

"Good-bye, Ned," said Mr. Chester.

"Good-bye, sir," said Ned. "I hope you get to Westchester without trouble."

"Good-bye, Ned," said George, and then he hit Ned on the arm.

"Good-bye, George," said Ned, "I'll hit you back when we meet again."

Ned headed down Broadway toward Wall Street. Must be something in my eye, he said to himself. Then he wiped the tears off his cheek.

As Ned went down Wall Street, he stopped at City Hall. Ned looked at the soldier by the door. Ned asked, "Is the General here?"

"You for the General or the King?" asked the soldier.

"We're not in it," said Ned, "we don't want to see a war."

"Then I don't guess I'll tell you where the General is. You might be a loyalist spy. You a spy, boy?"

Ned didn't know if the soldier was fooling with him or not. "I'm no spy," he said, "I'm a sailor."

"Then get on down to your ship," said the soldier. "A sailor is too dumb to be a spy."

Ned moved out into the street. "No sailor is dumb enough to be a soldier," he yelled. Then he ran for the East River.

Ned ran down Wall Street jumping over every little pig he saw. He had jumped over nine pigs when he stopped with his mouth open. The *London Lady* was tied up at Murray's Wharf.

"Ho, Luke," he shouted. "Why are you back so soon? Where's Father?" He stopped when he saw the funny look on Luke's face.

"Father's gone," Luke said. "The English took him. They stopped us and took him off. The dirty lobsterbacks impressed Father!"

Chapter 4
THE BATTLE FOR BROOKLYN

Ned and Luke sat on a pile of lumber at Murray's Wharf. American soldiers were getting into the *London Lady*. Ned felt a hand muss his hair. He looked up to see Jacob Smith smiling down at him.

"How are you, sailor?" asked Jacob. "Ready to sail these soldiers to Brooklyn?"

"Luke sails the *Lady*," said Ned. "I'm his helper."

"Let's go then," said Jacob. "I'm going to be with you. Sort of as a helper."

Ned, Luke, and Jacob made many trips that day. Each time they got to Brooklyn, men on the docks told them the news. The English had put 15,000 soldiers onto Long Island. Most were red-coated Englishmen. Some were blue-coated Hessians.

On the last trip to Brooklyn, the news was bad. The English were moving from their camps. "There will be fighting tomorrow," a soldier said. "August 27th—that is the day men will die."

"That was our last trip," said Jacob. "You boys sail the *Lady* back to the wharf."

"What will you do?" asked Ned.

"I'll find my Salem friends," said Jacob. "I want to be fighting tomorrow."

"Be careful," said Luke, "don't get killed."

"Don't get impressed," said Ned.

Jacob laughed. "I won't."

Luke and Ned sailed back to the wharf. They tied up the *Lady* and ate supper. Then they lay down and went to sleep.

"Please, God," said Ned before he closed his eyes. "Take care of Father and Jacob."

On August 27th the sun came up red and
angry. The English and the Hessians moved in
long lines at the Americans. The Americans
fired, reloaded, and fired again. English and
Hessian soldiers fell dead or hurt.

The lines of red and blue came closer to the
Americans. Then the English and Hessians were
fighting hand to hand with the Americans.

The English had bayonets—long knives—on
their guns. The English stabbed with their
bayonets. The Americans had no bayonets. They
swung their guns like clubs. More and more
Americans fell dead.

All along the line, the Americans moved back.
Soon many of them were running for Brooklyn.
By noon it was clear that the English had won.

The next morning it rained. Ned woke up. "Rain," he said as he shook Luke. "Get up, there's a bad storm coming."

"It isn't light yet," said Luke. He looked over at Brooklyn. "Let's sail to Brooklyn before the storm hits. Our side lost the fight yesterday. Maybe we can find Jacob, or even Father."

The trip over was a rough one. When they got to Brooklyn, it was raining hard. "Tie up the *Lady*," Luke said. "I'm going up into town. You stay here."

Ned stayed on the *Lady* all day. He wished Luke was back. Where was he? Had the English shot him? It was getting dark and still raining hard.

"Ho, Ned!" The call made Ned jump. He looked out to see Luke and Jacob running down the dock. Behind them were many men in blue coats. Ned yelled, "Look out for the Hessians."

"They aren't Hessians," said Jacob. "They are sailors from Marblehead. They are going to spend this night rowing."

"Why?" asked Ned.

"Because Washington is going to move all his men to New York City tonight."

"In this storm?"

"Right!" said Jacob. "The English won't see or hear a thing in the storm."

"And we are going to help move them," said Luke.

"We have made seven trips," said Ned.

"This is our last one," said Jacob. "The wind is almost stopped. We'll need luck to get back to New York."

"What about the rest of the soldiers?" Ned asked. "How will they get back?"

"Those Marblehead and Salem sailors can row all night," said Jacob. "They will get them all across the river."

Ned looked into the fog. He couldn't see more than a few feet from the *Lady*. But he could hear rowboats and voices.

"We fooled the English," someone said. "They don't even know we are gone."

"Six hours," someone else said. "We moved all of Washington's army in six hours. The army is safe in New York again."

KING'S BRID

FREE BRIDGE

FORT
WASHINGTON

NORTH OR HUDSON RIVER

KING'S BRIDGE ROAD

HARLEM R.

POINT
OF
ROCKS

FORT

BLOOMINGDALE ROAD

BLACKWELL'S ISLAND

KIPS BAY

EAST RIVER

NEW YORK

Chapter 5
THE BATTLE FOR NEW YORK CITY

Ned and Luke worked hard for the next four weeks. Jacob worked with them. They carried soldiers and gunpowder on the *Lady*.

They would sail up the East River. Then they would go up the Harlem River to the Free Bridge. The soldiers would take the gunpowder on to Fort Washington.

The Americans had 4,000 soldiers in New York. They had even more soldiers at Fort Washington.

On one trip, Jacob said, "Look at the redcoats digging on Blackwell's Island. There will be cannon in those holes soon."

"Will they shoot at us?" asked Ned.

"I don't think so," said Jacob. "They are getting ready to take men across the river."

"Look behind us!" Ned yelled. "The English are coming up the river."

"That means this is our last trip," said Jacob. "We can't sail back through those ships."

"What will we do?"

"We'll tie the *Lady* up at the Free Bridge. Then we'll go up to Fort Washington. Someone up there will tell us what to do."

"We won't lose the *Lady*, will we?"

"No," said Jacob. "We will sail the *Lady* up to Boston if we have to. There are no English up there now."

That night Ned and Jacob slept at Fort Washington. Luke had stayed with the *Lady*. The soldiers at the fort said there would be fighting soon.

The next morning Jacob found his friends from Salem. "I have to stay with them now," said Jacob. "You can stay with me until the fighting begins."

Ned was happy to stay with Jacob. It was almost as good as being with Father. The Salem soldiers had a camp at a place called Point of Rocks. It was on high ground and Ned could see for miles.

It was a hot, clear day. Ned was looking at Blackwell's Island when he heard the boom of cannon. Boom! Boom! Boom! The cannon went on and on.

"Sounds like the English landed at Kip's Bay," said Jacob. "That's miles from here."

Ned was eating his lunch when he saw the soldiers. "Look," he said to Jacob, "here come our soldiers!"

Ned watched the soldiers climb the hill. Most of them asked for water. Ned ran from man to man. Each dipped a cup of water from Ned's pail.

"Did we win?" asked Ned.

"We lost," said a soldier. "We had to run from the redcoats."

"The cannon," said another, "it was the cannon that did it. We couldn't stand against the cannon. It was run or die at Kip's Bay."

More and more men came up the hill. Ned heard them say the English were moving north.

That means they are coming here, Ned thought. Why do we always lose to the English?

Late that afternoon, Ned saw the red line of men. They were moving up the Kings Bridge Road. Then he saw the dust on the west road. Soon he could see brown coats. "Jacob," Ned called. "Look down there."

Jacob looked. "It's a race," he said. "The English are coming up one road. Our soldiers from New York are coming up the other."

"Can they see each other?" asked Ned.

"I don't think so," said Jacob. "There is a mile or two of woods between them. But it is a life or death race for our men."

The two groups of men came up the roads. The Americans were moving fast. The English didn't seem to be in any hurry. "The redcoats can't see them," Ned said. Soon the Americans were climbing the hills.

Ned pointed at the English. "They didn't see you," he said. An American looked and then shook his head.

"We didn't know they were there," he said.

It was still dark when Ned woke up. He could hear soldiers moving. "What is it?" he asked.

"It's the Connecticut Rangers," said Jacob. "They are headed for the English lines."

As the sun came up, Ned watched the Rangers. They began to shoot at the English. The fight was about even. Then more English came up. The Rangers began to fall back. We are going to lose again, Ned thought.

"Look over there," said Jacob. "There come men from Massachusetts and Virginia. The Rangers aren't losing. They are drawing the redcoats into a trap."

The fighting began again. Down the hill went more men from Virginia and Maryland. The English began to fall back. Ned could hear the Americans yelling at the English.

"We're winning!" Ned yelled. "This time we're winning!"

"We had to win this time," said Jacob. "We had to show the English we can fight."

"Did we win a big battle? Have we won the war?"

"No," said Jacob. "It was a small battle. All it shows is that we can stand and fight."

Chapter 6
NEW YORK . . . GOOD-BYE

It was October. Ned and Jacob were back on the *Lady*. With Luke, they had sailed up to Pell's Point. Their job was to spy on the English. If they saw ships coming, they were to sail into the bay and tell the Americans.

"If we sail into the bay," asked Ned, "how will we get away? The English ships will trap us in there."

"We will get close to land," said Jacob. "We will hide until night and then sail away."

On October 12th they heard the English had landed far to the south. A group of Pennsylvania soldiers stopped them there.

"Keep your eyes open, lads," said Jacob. "The English can't move by land down south. That means they will try up here soon."

"I wish Father were here," said Ned. "He could get hurt on an English ship."

"I miss him too," said Luke. "It has been three months since we saw him."

Things were quiet for a week. Then on the 18th, they saw the English ships. Luke turned the *Lady* and sailed for Pell's Point.

Luke sailed the ship up to the dock at the Point. "Get ready to fight," he yelled.

"Let's get out of here," Jacob said. "Try to get around the Point."

"This is like another race," said Ned. "But this time we are in it."

"We can't get around the Point," Jacob said. "Run the *Lady* close to shore and go up that little bay."

The English ships sailed past them. Redcoated soldiers began to go ashore. "We're little fish," said Luke. "They can get us later if they want to."

The sun went down. The sounds of fighting stopped. Soon it was dark.

"Shhh," said Jacob, "I hear something coming."

Ned could hear something moving on the water. It was a small boat of some kind. The men in it were trying to be quiet. They are after us, Ned thought.

Then Ned could hear a voice, "We'll go up here as far as we can. Then we'll walk across the point."

Ned jumped up and yelled, "Father! We're over here, Father! The *Lady's* right here!"

The small boat moved to the *Lady's* side. Then Father and another man were on her deck. Father fell to his knees and hugged Ned and Luke. He shook hands with Jacob.

"We were on one of the English ships," he said. "We were rowing the redcoats to shore. When it got dark, we just rowed off."

"Father," said Ned, "Luke and I are rebels now."

"I guess the English made all of us into rebels," said Father. "But New York City now belongs to the English army. We'll sail up to Boston or Salem."

"I'd like to see Salem," said Ned. "Jacob is from Salem."

"All right," said Father. "We'll sail to Salem. Ned, Luke, go forward. Jacob, push off from the shore!"

"Good-bye, New York," said Ned. "We'll be back when you are an American city again."

EPILOGUE

It was more than six years before the Americans came back to New York City. The English held the city all through the war and for two more years until a peace treaty was signed in 1783.

The English soldiers didn't take care of the city during the war. They cut down the trees for firewood. They used the churches for hospitals. They used some buildings for prisons. They built no new houses. The streets became full of garbage and junk. When the Americans came back into the city, they had to rebuild many of the houses and stores.

After New York City was rebuilt, it became the capital of the United States. The Congress met there, and the first President, George Washington, lived in the city.

IMPORTANT DATES OF THE REVOLUTION

1775	April 19	Fighting at Lexington and Concord
	May 10	Ethan Allen captures Fort Ticonderoga
	June 15	George Washington elected commander-in-chief of army
	June 16/17	Battle of Bunker (Breed's) Hill;
	September	American soldiers invade Canada; Ethan Allen captured
	November/ December	British and Americans fight in Canada, South Carolina, New York, Virginia, Maine, and at sea
1776	March 17	British withdraw from Boston
	July 4	Congress adopts the Declaration of Independence
	August 27	Battle of Long Island; Americans retreat
	September 15	British take New York City
	September 16	Americans win Battle of Harlem Heights
	October 11/13	British fleet wins Battle of Lake Champlain
	October 28	British win at White Plains, N. Y.
	November 16	British take Fort Washington
	November 28	British take Rhode Island
	December	Washington takes army across Delaware and into Pennsylvania
	December 26	Washington wins Battle of Trenton, New Jersey
1777	January 3	Americans win Battle of Princeton
	January	American army winters at Morristown, New Jersey
	August 6	Battle of Oriskany, N. Y.
	August 16	Americans win Battle of Bennington, Vt.
	September 11	British win Battle of Brandywine
	September 26	British occupy Philadelphia
	October 4	British win Battle of Germantown
	October 6	British capture Forts Clinton and Montgomery
	October 7	Battles of Saratoga, N. Y.; British General Burgoyne's army surrenders October 17
	November 15	Articles of Confederation adopted
	December 18	Washington's army winters at Valley Forge

1778	February 6	France signs treaty of alliance with America
	June 18	British evacuate Philadelphia
	June 28	Americans win Battle of Monmouth Court House, N.J.
	July 4	George Rogers Clark wins at Kaskaskia
	August 29	Battle of Rhode Island; Americans retreat
	December 29	British capture Savannah, Ga.
1779	January	British take Vincennes, Ind.
	February 3	British lose at Charles Town, S. C.
	February 14	Americans win at Kettle Creek, Ga.
	February 20	Americans capture Vincennes
	March 3	British win at Briar Creek, Ga.
	June 20	Americans lose at Stono Ferry, S.C.
	July 16	Americans take Fort Stony Point, N. Y.
	August/ September	Fighting continues on land and sea. On September 23 John Paul Jones captures British *Serapis*
	December	Americans winter at Morristown, N.J.
1780	May 12	Charles Town surrenders to British
	June 20	Battle of Ramsour's Mills, N. C.
	July 30	Battle of Rocky Mount, S. C.
	September 26	Battle of Charlotte, N. C.
	October 7	Battle of King's Mountain, S. C.
1781	January 17	Americans win Battle of Cowpens, S. C.
	March/April	Battles in North Carolina, South Carolina, Virginia, Georgia
	October 19	British army surrenders at Yorktown
1782	July 11	British leave Savannah, Ga.
	November 30	Preliminary peace signed between America and Britain
	December 14	British leave Charleston, S. C.
1783	September 3	Final peace treaty signed
	November 25	British evacuate New York City

About the Authors:

Susan Dye Lee has been writing professionally since she graduated from college in 1961. Working with the Social Studies Curriculum Center at Northwestern University, she has created course materials in American studies. Ms. Lee has also co-authored a text on Latin America and Canada, written case studies in legal history for the Law in American Society Project, and developed a teacher's guide for tapes that explore women's role in America's past. The writer credits her students for many of her ideas. Currently, she is doing research for her history dissertation on the Women's Christian Temperance Union for Northwestern University. In her free moments, Susan Lee enjoys traveling, playing the piano, and welcoming friends to "Highland Cove," the summer cottage she and her husband, John, share.

John R. Lee enjoys a prolific career as a writer, teacher, and outdoorsman. After receiving his doctorate in social studies at Stanford, Dr. Lee came to Northwestern University's School of Education, where he advises student teachers and directs graduates in training. A versatile writer, Dr. Lee has co-authored the Scott-Foresman social studies textbooks for primary-age children. In addition, he has worked on the production of 50 films and over 100 filmstrips. His biographical film on Helen Keller received a 1970 Venice Film Festival award. His college text, *Teaching Social Studies in the Elementary School*, has recently been published. Besides pro-football, Dr. Lee's passion is his Wisconsin cottage, where he likes to shingle leaky roofs, split wood, and go sailing.

About the Artist:

Tom Dunnington divides his time between book illustration and wildlife painting. He has done many books for Childrens Press, as well as working on textbooks, and is a regular contributor to "Highlights for Children." He is at present working on his "Endangered Wildlife" series, which is being reproduced as limited edition prints. Tom lives in Elmhurst.

The Bat...
and New York

Date Due

Rm 10			
Rm 9			
Rm 8			

Lee, Susan
LEE   The Battle for Long Island
         and New York